CLIFF LEE

Michelle Medlock Adams

South Huntington Pub. Lib.
145 Pidgeon Hill Rd.
Huntington Sta., N.Y. 11746

Mitchell Lane
PUBLISHERS

P.O. Box 196
Hockessin, Delaware 19707
Visit us on the web: www.mitchelllane.com
Comments? email us: mitchelllane@mitchelllane.com

Copyright © 2012 by Mitchell Lane Publishers. All rights reserved. No part of this book may be reproduced without written permission from the publisher. Printed and bound in the United States of America.

Printing   1   2   3   4   5   6   7   8   9

A Robbie Reader Biography

Abigail Breslin	Dr. Seuss	Mia Hamm
Adrian Peterson	Dwayne "The Rock" Johnson	Miley Cyrus
Albert Einstein	Dwyane Wade	Miranda Cosgrove
Albert Pujols	Dylan & Cole Sprouse	Philo Farnsworth
Alex Rodriguez	Eli Manning	Raven-Symoné
Aly and AJ	Emily Osment	Roy Halladay
AnnaSophia Robb	Emma Watson	Selena Gomez
Amanda Bynes	Hilary Duff	Shaquille O'Neal
Ashley Tisdale	Jaden Smith	Story of Harley-Davidson
Brenda Song	Jamie Lynn Spears	Sue Bird
Brittany Murphy	Jennette McCurdy	Syd Hoff
Charles Schulz	Jesse McCartney	Taylor Lautner
Chris Johnson	Jimmie Johnson	Tiki Barber
Cliff Lee	Johnny Gruelle	Tim Lincecum
Dakota Fanning	Jonas Brothers	Tom Brady
Dale Earnhardt Jr.	Jordin Sparks	Tony Hawk
David Archuleta	Justin Beiber	Troy Polamalu
Demi Lovato	Keke Palmer	Victoria Justice
Donovan McNabb	Larry Fitzgerald	
Drake Bell & Josh Peck	LeBron James	

Library of Congress Cataloging-in-Publication Data
Adams, Michelle Medlock.
  Cliff Lee / by Michelle Medlock Adams.
     p. cm. — (A Robbie reader)
  Includes bibliographical references and index.
  ISBN 978-1-61228-065-3 (library bound)
 1. Lee, Cliff, 1978– —Juvenile literature. 2. Baseball players—United States—Biography—Juvenile literature. 3. Pitchers (Baseball)—United States—Biography—Juvenile literature. I. Title.
  GV865.L364A43 2012
  796.357092—dc22
  [B]
                                                                                            2011016784
eBook ISBN: 9781612281773

ABOUT THE AUTHOR: Michelle Medlock Adams is an award-winning writer, earning top honors from the Associated Press, the Society of Professional Journalists and the Hoosier State Press Association. Author of 44 books, she has also written thousands of articles for newspapers, web sites, and magazines since graduating with a journalism degree from Indiana University. Michelle, her husband, Jeff, and their two daughters, Abby and Ally, reside in Southern Indiana, where they cheer for the Bedford North Lawrence Stars, the Indiana University Hoosiers, the Chicago Cubs, and the Indianapolis Colts. To find out more about Michelle, visit her web site at http://www.michellemedlockadams.com.

PUBLISHER'S NOTE: The following story has been thoroughly researched and to the best of our knowledge represents a true story. While every possible effort has been made to ensure accuracy, the publisher will not assume liability for damages caused by inaccuracies in the data, and makes no warranty on the accuracy of the information contained herein. This story has not been authorized or endorsed by Cliff Lee.

                                                                                            PLB

TABLE OF CONTENTS

Chapter One
Victories to Celebrate 5

Chapter Two
An Ace Is Born 9

Chapter Three
Family First 13

Chapter Four
Making His Mark 17

Chapter Five
Back Home in Philly 23

Chronology 28
Career Statistics 29
Find Out More 29
    Books 29
    Works Consulted 29
    On the Internet 30
Glossary 31
Index 32

Words in **bold** type can be found in the glossary.

Cliff Lee hurls a pitch against the Yankees on a cold October night in the Bronx, New York, during Game 3 of the American League Championship Series in 2010.

CHAPTER ONE

Victories to Celebrate

Just past midnight following one of the biggest baseball games of his life, star pitcher Cliff Lee sat next to his nine-year-old son, Jaxon, in the Texas Rangers' clubhouse. Cliff dropped his towel into the laundry bin as if he had just pitched in any old game during any old baseball season, but that was far from the truth.

Cliff Lee made history that October night in 2010 when the Rangers beat the New York Yankees 8-0. He had gone eight innings, allowing only two hits and no runs. This put his team ahead two games to one in the American League Championship Series. Lee became the first man to strike out 10-plus hitters in three straight starts during the same postseason play.

5

Lee and his son, Jaxon, ride in the All-Star parade in 2008.

It was a first in the history of baseball, and an **accomplishment** (uh-KOM-plish-munt) to celebrate. Yet Lee seemed much more interested in kicking back with his son and enjoying a little father-son time on this very important night. That confused many sportswriters, who were hounding Lee with questions about his historic night of pitching. As he left the clubhouse, he simply smiled and said he had been told of his achievement. Then he continued walking toward his vehicle with Jaxon by his side.

Maybe some of those reporters had forgotten that Jaxon had been diagnosed with cancer when he was only four months old and given only a 30 percent chance to live. Jaxon spent four months going through **chemotherapy** (kee-moh-THAYR-uh-pee) and other treatments, fighting for his life. By his first birthday, he was cancer free.

While the sports world **marveled** at Lee's hard work and his achievement, Lee marveled at the fact that his son had fought cancer, won, and lived to celebrate such a special moment with him. For Lee, that was the sweetest victory.

Lee has become one of the best left-handed pitchers in the majors.

CHAPTER TWO

An Ace Is Born

Clifton Phifer "Cliff" Lee was born on August 30, 1978, in Benton, Arkansas, to Steve and Sharon Lee. The name they gave him carries great family importance. His first name, Clifton, is the first name of his maternal grandfather (his mother's father), and his middle name is his mother's maiden name (her last name before she married Cliff's father).

Proud papa Steve Lee, a firefighter at the time, had no idea that the baby boy he held in his arms would one day win the most **prestigious** (preh-STIH-jus) awards in Major League Baseball, but baby Cliff grew up believing in his **destiny** (DES-tih-nee).

CHAPTER TWO

When he was only about nine years old, Cliff told his father that he wanted to be a major league pitcher. He had a great role model because his American Legion baseball coach, Wes Gardner, had been a major league pitcher for the Boston Red Sox.

Cliff in his high school yearbook

As a left-handed pitcher, Cliff shined at the high school level. In fact, he was **drafted** his senior year by the Florida Marlins, but they could not agree on all the contract terms. Instead, Cliff signed with the University of Arkansas at Little Rock, a Division I team. However, he found out that Division I players cannot be drafted until after their junior year. Not wanting to delay his chances for the big league, he switched to Meridian Community College in Mississippi.

Cliff in his Arkansas uniform

10

AN ACE IS BORN

Cliff as a Meridian Eagle

In the year 2000, Lee signed with the University of Arkansas. He pitched one season for that team before the Montreal Expos drafted him in the fourth round. That was a big year for Lee, as it was also the year he married his childhood friend, Kristen. They had known each other since she was in sixth grade and he was in seventh. Over the years, their friendship **blossomed** into love, and that love continues today.

Cliff and his wife, Kristen, with son Jaxon and daughter Maci

Lee would face the challenge of spring training with the Indians in 2003, but that would not be his biggest challenge that year.

CHAPTER THREE

Family First

Everything was going right for Lee. He had been promoted to the Jupiter Hammerheads of the Class-A Florida State League for the 2001 season. On April 29, he and Kristen welcomed a son into the world. It seemed as if life could not get any better for the Lees.

Their joy soon turned to sadness and fear when they learned their son, Jaxon, had a form of cancer called **acute myelogenous leukemia** (uh-KYOOT my-uh-LAH-juh-nus loo-KEE-mee-uh). During the Hammerheads' final weekend of play, Kristen and Jaxon visited Cliff in Florida. Jaxon became very sick with a fever and vomiting. At first, hospital doctors thought

CHAPTER THREE

the infant had an infection, but further testing revealed leukemia. Jaxon was only four months old.

"Seeing your child almost die is the second-worst thing that can happen, next to losing your child," Kristen told a reporter in 2002.

"That was a definite shock," Cliff shared in the same interview. "It was pretty bad the first couple of days, but after

Dr. Robert Saylors of the Arkansas Children's Hospital stands with Cliff Lee and his family in a photo taken after Jaxon (right) was pronounced cancer free. Cliff donated $1 million to the hospital.

FAMILY FIRST

that it's just like . . . What do we need to do to get this taken care of?"

With that determined attitude, the Lees flew home to Arkansas. Jaxon had chemotherapy and eventually **radiation** (ray-dee-AY-shun) treatments at the Arkansas Children's Hospital in Little Rock. In January 2002, they took Jaxon to San Antonio for a **stem cell** transplant. He has been in remission (ree-MIH-shun)—or winning the battle against cancer—ever since. For the whole Lee family, life began to take a turn for the better once again.

On April 5, 2003, the Lees welcomed a daughter, Maci, into the world. Cliff spent most of that year pitching in the minors in Buffalo, New York, for the Bisons. He pitched well, but he was not **consistent** (kun-SIS-tent). An **abdominal** (ub-DAH-mih-nul) injury was affecting his pitching. Even so, in mid-August, he went to Cleveland and claimed a regular spot playing for the Indians.

Lee on the Bisons team

In Game 1 of the 2009 World Series, Lee did not surrender even one earned run to the New York Yankees in a complete game victory for him and the Philadelphia Phillies.

CHAPTER FOUR

Making His Mark

The years with the Cleveland Indians were filled with ups and downs for Lee. Despite the lows, he was definitely making his mark in the professional baseball world. In fact, in 2008 he won the Cy Young Award for being the best pitcher in the American League.

In July 2009, Lee was traded to the Philadelphia Phillies. The Lees felt at home in Philly, but their stay was short-lived. In December, he was traded to the Seattle Mariners and traded again in July 2010 to the Texas Rangers.

The 2010 season held many career **highlights** for Lee. He was named the

CHAPTER FOUR

American League Pitcher of the Month for June and was selected to the American League All-Star Team on July 4. Two weeks later, on July 22, he got his 1,000th career major league strikeout when he struck out Torii Hunter of the Los Angeles Angels. On August 6, he earned his 100th career major league victory. And he was selected to the Arkansas Sports Hall of Fame class of 2011.

That year, the Rangers won every game as the away team in the postseason playoffs. It was a first in major league history. Lee's win on October 12 was the first in the streak. He also set a record when he became the first pitcher in major league history to reach double digits in strikeouts three times in a single postseason.

Lee pitched in two of the seven games of the 2010 World Series. While facing the San Francisco Giants in Game 1, he struggled a bit. The game was tied until the fifth inning when the Giants scored six runs.

In a postgame interview, Lee expressed his disappointment. "I was trying to make

On October 18, 2010, Lee returned to postseason baseball in the Bronx and again had the Yankees on their knees, allowing not a single earned run in eight innings.

CHAPTER FOUR

adjustments," he said. "I was up. I was down. I was in. I was out. I was trying to find it, and I was never really consistent with what I was doing."

The Rangers lost that game 11-7.

Then in Game 5, Lee pitched again. The Giants won 3-1, winning the World Series four games to one.

Lee is also an outstanding fielder and hitter. He made a spectacular diving play on a bunt during Game 5 of the 2010 World Series.

The season hadn't ended as he'd hoped, but Lee kept looking forward. In November, the Benton Area Chamber of Commerce named him and Kristen Citizen of the Year for their charity work. They had done a lot for their community: They bought state championship rings for the Benton High School baseball team. They gave money and time to the Miracle League, which gives children with disabilities the chance to play baseball. They also made donations to the Leukemia & **Lymphoma** (lim-FOH-muh) Society and other causes.

Also in November, Cliff was granted free agency. That meant his agent could meet with various teams to try to get him the best contract possible. Lee considered offers from the New York Yankees, the Texas Rangers, and several other teams.

Lee shocked the baseball world by turning down the Yankees to sign with the Phillies, even though New York offered him more money.

CHAPTER
FIVE

Back Home in Philly

Lee had a tough choice to make. Some teams offered him more money. Some offered him a longer contract. And some offered him a better chance to win a World Series. In the end, the decision was easy—Philadelphia. Lee had gotten a taste of the super-charged Philly baseball world when he played for them in 2009. He took them to the World Series that year, pitching two winning games against the Yankees. The fans loved him for it! When Lee was traded to Seattle just 42 days after that season, he left Philly feeling as if he had unfinished business there. Now he had the chance to finish that business, and Philly fans were thrilled.

CHAPTER FIVE

The "four aces" of the Phillies, left to right: Roy Halladay, Roy Oswalt, Cliff Lee, and Cole Hamels. By midseason in 2011, they had more shutouts (12) than any group of Phillies pitchers since 1964.

Lee could see plenty of victories in the Phillies' future. With its stellar pitching staff, 2011 could be a magical year. When he signed with the Phillies, he became one of the "four aces"—Cliff Lee, Roy Halladay, Roy Oswalt, and Cole Hamels. Baseball fans and sportswriters predicted that the team would go all the way to the World Series.

Lee likes winning, but he also loves the guys on the team—especially Halladay and his

BACK HOME IN PHILLY

other fellow pitchers. "I never wanted to leave in the first place," he said in a preseason press conference. "To get an opportunity to come back and be part of this team and this pitching rotation is going to be something that's historic, I believe."

Kristen and the Lee children also love Philly. "I would have never dreamed . . . that we would say, 'Ooh, Philadelphia, I can't wait to get there,' " Kristen said. "But it's a city like

A tale of two cities: Newspaper headlines showed the outrage in New York (left), and the joy in Philadelphia (right).

Halfway through the 2011 season, Lee was in the National League top five in strikeouts and ERA, and had a consecutive scoreless innings streak going at 32 straight.

I've never been in before. We haven't had that exact feeling anywhere else."

Lee signed a five-year deal for $120 million. It was far less than the $132 million over six years that the Yankees had put on the table.

"It's plenty of money," Cliff said about his decision. "When you hit a certain point, enough's enough. . . . At this point, it's about trying to win championships [and] I think this team gives me the best chance to do that."

Lee and his fans are happy he is back in Philadelphia. Shortly after he signed with Philly, Lee dined in a steakhouse in his old neighborhood, and the customers stood up and clapped for him. Local T-shirt companies started making shirts that said, "Cliff Lee Is Back!"

"I never held any grudges for being traded," he told a local reporter. "From the day I got here, I knew it was something special. I didn't know I would have an opportunity to come back."

CHRONOLOGY

1978 Clifton Phifer "Cliff" Lee is born on August 30 in Benton, Arkansas.

1987 Cliff tells his father that he wants to be a major league pitcher someday.

1997 He is drafted his senior year by the Florida Marlins, but they cannot agree on contract terms. Lee signs with the University of Arkansas at Little Rock but quickly switches to Meridian Community College in Mississippi.

2000 Lee signs with the University of Arkansas and pitches one season. Montreal drafts him in the fourth round. Cliff marries his childhood friend, Kristen.

2001 Lee is promoted to the Jupiter Hammerheads. He and Kristen welcome baby Jaxon on April 29. When he is four months old, Jaxon is diagnosed with cancer.

2002 Jaxon undergoes a stem cell transplant in January and goes into remission.

2003 The Lees welcome their daughter, Maci, into the world on April 5. Cliff claims a regular spot playing for the Cleveland Indians by mid-August.

2008 Lee wins the American League Cy Young Award.

2009 He is traded to the Philadelphia Phillies. In December, he is traded to the Seattle Mariners.

2010 He is traded to the Texas Rangers in July, and achieves his 1,000th career major league strikeout on July 22. He is selected to the Arkansas Sports Hall of Fame class of 2011. He makes his second World Series appearance in October, but the Texas Rangers still lose to the San Francisco Giants. Cliff and Kristen are named Citizen of the Year by the Benton Area Chamber of Commerce for their charity work. Cliff signs a five-year deal with the Phillies for $120 million on December 14.

2011 In May, Lee helps the Phillies beat the visiting Cincinnati Reds, becoming the first Phillies pitcher to drive in three runs in a game since Cory Lidle did so in 2004. Also, Lee shuts out the Texas Rangers, 2-0 – the team he helped lead to the World Series the year before. Lee goes 5-0 in June, giving up just one run the entire month, and pitches three straight complete game shutouts for the Phillies. He is the first pitcher to do that for the team since Robin Roberts in 1950.

CAREER STATISTICS

Year	Team	GS	W	L	IP	H	ER	HR	BB	CG	K	ERA
2002	Cleveland	2	0	1	10.1	6	2	0	8	0	6	1.74
2003	Cleveland	9	3	3	52.1	41	21	7	20	0	44	3.61
2004	Cleveland	33	14	8	179.0	188	108	30	81	0	161	5.43
2005	Cleveland	32	18	5	202.0	194	85	22	52	1	143	3.79
2006	Cleveland	33	14	11	200.2	224	98	29	58	1	129	4.40
2007	Cleveland	16	5	8	97.1	112	68	17	36	1	66	6.29
2008	Cleveland	31	22	3	223.1	214	63	12	34	4	170	2.54
2009	Cleveland	22	7	9	152.0	165	53	10	33	3	107	3.14
2009	Phillies	12	7	4	79.2	80	30	7	10	3	74	3.39
2010	Seattle	13	8	3	103.2	92	27	5	6	5	89	2.34
2010	Texas	15	4	6	108.2	103	48	11	12	2	96	3.98
Career		218	102	61	1406.2	1419	603	150	350	20	1085	3.70

GS = Games Started, W = Wins, L = Losses, IP = Innings Pitched, H = Hits, ER = Earned Runs, HR = Home Runs Allowed, BB = Bases on Balls, CG = Complete Games, K = Strikeouts, ERA = Earned Run Average

FIND OUT MORE

Books
Basen, Ryan. *Texas Rangers* (Inside MLB). Edina, MN: SportsZONE, 2011.
Gagne, Tammy. *Roy Halladay.* Hockessin, DE: Mitchell Lane Publishers, 2012.
Jackson, Dave. *Philadelphia Phillies* (Inside MLB). Edina, MN: SportsZONE, 2011.
Jacobs, Greg. *The Everything Kids' Baseball Book: From Baseball History to Player Stats—With Lots of Homerun Fun in Between!* Avon, MA: Adams Media, 2010.

Works Consulted
The Associated Press and Jerry Crasnick. "Cliff Lee Never Wanted to Leave Phils." *ESPN News,* December 15, 2010. http://sports.espn.go.com/mlb/news/story?id=5923327
Baseball Reference: Cliff Lee Statistics
http://www.baseball-reference.com/players/l/leecl02.shtml
Brantley, Max. "Cliff Lee Family Gives $1 Million to Children's." *Arkansas Times,* November 23, 2010. http://www.arktimes.com/ArkansasBlog/archives/2010/11/23/cliff-lee-family-gives-1-million-to-childrens
Chandler, Rick. "Was Son's Health a Factor in the Cliff Lee Decision?" NBC Sports/Off the Bench, December 14, 2010. http://offthebench.nbcsports.com/2010/12/14/was-sons-health-a-factor-in-the-cliff-lee-decision/
Cook, Marty. "Lee's Full Focus on Family Now." *Arkansas Democrat-Gazette,* June 17, 2002. http://www.hognation.net/bios/leestories.html
Durrett, Richard, and Andrew Marchand. "Yankees, Rangers Chase Cliff Lee." *ESPN Sports,* December 7, 2010. http://sports.espn.go.com/dallas/mlb/news/story?id=5891606

Gelston, Dan. "Lee Set for First Start vs. Rangers." *Yahoo! Sports,* May 20, 2011. http://sports.yahoo.com/mlb/news?slug=ap-phillies-lee

Harris, Jim. "Cliff Lee: A Comeback Even Cy Young Would Applaud." *Arkansas Sports,* January 5, 2009. http://www.arkansassports360.com/12953/cliff-lee-a-comeback-even-cy-young-would-applaud

Jockbios: Cliff Lee's Biography. http://www.jockbio.com/Bios/Cl_Lee/Cl_Lee_bio.html

King, Harry. "Friend Shares Story of Cliff Lee's Workout." May 28, 2008. http://thecabin.net/stories/052808/spo_0528080025.shtml

Lemire, Joe. "Three Things We Learned from Cliff Lee's New Deal with Philadelphia." *Sports Illustrated,* December 14, 2010. http://sportsillustrated.cnn.com/2010/writers/joe_lemire/12/14/lee.to.phillies/index.html

Marchand, Andrew. "Cliff Lee's Wife Harassed in New York." *ESPN Sports,* October 27, 2010. http://sports.espn.go.com/new-york/mlb/news/story?id=5729471

Morosi, Jon Paul. "Lee Humble After Masterful Performance." *Fox Sports,* October 19, 2010. http://msn.foxsports.com/mlb/story/Cliff-Lee-humble-after-throwing-postseason-masterpiece-vs-Yankees-101810

Player Wives: "Kristen Lee." October 26, 2010. http://www.playerwives.com/mlb/cleveland-indians/cliff-lees-wife-kristen-lee/

SportsDayDFW. "Cliff Lee's Personality Doesn't Favor the Big City; Friend Hopes He Stays with Rangers." *Dallas News,* November 15, 2010. http://rangersblog.dallasnews.com/archives/2010/11/cliff-lees-personality-doesnt.html

Starkey, J.P. "Cliff Lee Pitches Rangers to ALCS Lead and into Record Books." *SB Nation,* October 18, 2010. http://dallas.sbnation.com/texas-rangers/2010/10/18/1759121/alcs-game-3-cliff-lee-rangers-look-to-take-alcs-lead

Townsend, Brad. "Meet Cliff Lee: The Man Who Saved the Rangers (and His Wife Likes Being Close to Texas)." *The Dallas Morning News,* October 18, 2010. http://www.dallasnews.com/sports/texas-rangers/headlines/20101017-Meet-Cliff-Lee-The-man-6168.ece

———. "Surprise Trade to Texas a Rewarding Experience for Rangers' Cliff Lee." *The Dallas Morning News,* October 18, 2010. http://www.txcn.com/sharedcontent/dws/dn/latestnews/stories/101810dnspo1aleelede_hp.1a1d13d6e.html

On the Internet

Cliff Lee—News, Photos, Topics, and Quotes
http://www.daylife.com/topic/Cliff_Lee

MLB: Cliff Lee
http://mlb.mlb.com/team/player.jsp?player_id=424324

PHOTO CREDITS: Cover, pp. 1, 22—Drew Hallowell/Getty Images; p. 4—Travis Lindquist/Getty Images; pp. 8, 27—Miles Kennedy/Getty Images; p. 12—Rick Stewart/Stringer/Getty Images; p. 16—Jim McIsaac/Getty Images; p. 19—Nick Laham/Getty Images; p. 20—David J. Phillip/AP Photo; all other photos—cc-by-sa-2.0. Every effort has been made to locate all copyright holders of materials used in this book. Any errors or omissions will be corrected in future editions of the book.

GLOSSARY

abdominal (ub-DAH-mih-nul)—In the stomach area.

accomplishment (uh-KOM-plish-munt)—A success; a goal that has been reached.

acute myelogenous leukemia (uh-KYOOT my-uh-LAH-juh-nus loo-KEE-mee-uh)—A type of cancer.

blossom (BLAH-sum)—To develop and bloom.

chemotherapy (kee-moh-THAYR-uh-pee)—A common treatment using strong chemicals to kill cancerous tissue.

consistent (kun-SIS-tunt)—Doing something the same way all the time.

destiny (DES-tih-nee)—Something that is supposed to happen.

draft (DRAFT)—To choose a new player.

highlight (HY-lyt)—An event to remember and celebrate.

lymphoma (lim-FOH-muh)—A type of cancer that causes growths to form on the parts of the body called lymph nodes.

marvel (MAR-vul)—To view with wonder or admiration.

pinstripe (PIN-stryp)—One of the thin stripes on fabric, such as on a baseball uniform.

prestigious (pre-STIH-jus)—Highly honored.

radiation (ray-dee-AY-shun)—A medical process used to treat cancer.

stem cell—A cell the human body can use to make specialized cells.

INDEX

American League 4, 17, 18
American League All-Star 18
American League Championship 4, 5
Arkansas Sports Hall of Fame 18
Benton Area Chamber of Commerce 21
Benton, Arkansas 9
Benton High School baseball 21
Buffalo Bisons 15
cancer 7, 13, 15
chemotherapy 7, 15
Cleveland Indians 12, 15, 17
Cy Young Award 17
Division I 10
Florida Marlins 10
Gardner, Wes 10
Halladay, Roy 24
Hamels, Cole 24
Jupiter Hammerheads 13
Lee, Cliff
    achievements 5, 7, 16, 18, 19, 26
    awards 9, 17, 18, 21
    birth 9
    charity 21
    contracts 21, 23, 27
draft 10
education 10–11
injury 15
Lee, Jaxon (son) 5, 6, 7, 11, 13, 14
Lee, Kristen (wife) 11, 13–14, 21, 25
Lee, Maci (daughter) 11, 14, 15
Lee, Sharon (mother) 9
Lee, Steve (father) 9
leukemia 13, 14, 21
Meridian Community College 10
Miracle League 21
Montreal Expos 11
New York Yankees 4, 5, 16, 19, 21, 22, 25, 27
Oswalt, Roy 23
Philadelphia Phillies 16, 17, 22, 23, 24, 25, 27
San Francisco Giants 18, 20
Saylor, Robert 14
Seattle Mariners 17
Texas Rangers 5, 17, 18, 20, 21, 22
University of Arkansas 10, 11
World Series 16, 18–21, 23, 24

FEB 1 6 2012

25 70